Dear Dan, of

Sorry you misse_ your day in court!

May your return trip to P.G. be fun!

P.S. Invite me to
your pig roast next year

778-999-2654

The Rose Possessed

KIRSTEN BRAWN-GOOD

Tellwell Talent
www.tellwell.ca

ISBN
978-1-77370-559-0 (Hardcover)
978-1-77962-072-9 (Paperback)

Dedication

I am deeply grateful to God, or the All-Seeing Eye, or maybe it's aliens, and I dedicate this book to his/their ever-present spirit in my life and the lives of those people around me and beyond.

Acknowledgements

I would like to acknowledge the importance of the late guitar genius, Eddie Van Halen, to my work. Though we had never been introduced, with him I felt a spiritual bonding, and he was the muse of many of my poems.

I would also like to thank my sister Gayle for her tremendous assistance in the editing of my manuscript. It was so wonderful to have her by my side.

About the Author

Kirsten Brawn has been a songwriter, ad copywriter, financial advisor and is now a poet, too.

In the beginning, she was a songwriter. Since elementary school, and like fishing from the stream, she's been receiving from the ether, words with rhythm and melody.

Of course, it's hard to make a living as a songwriter, even if you're good. So, after a stint as a finance person, she has harnessed the right side of her brain again and resides now in the grand sea of poetry.

Well, the poetry swimming around in the inspiration-sphere has met its fishing net. And, in "The Rose Possessed," Kirsten is serving it all up crisp and juicy.

Table of Contents

The Seedling

There is a jungle canopy, tall forest giants of
evergreen. Soaking up the light.
They grow bigger and stronger, their boughs grow longer,
they rule with their mighty height.

Somewhere below on the jungle floor is a seedling
trying to aspire.
As she gropes and fumbles in the woodland dirt, the
mighty trees grow higher.

The other seedlings in her reach, an astounding
multitude.
Struggle for any shard of light that could be their
growing food.

So many roots that just won't take. Without sun and
water, they suffocate.
Their ambition and talents lost for good, decayed in
the hungry giants' wood.

The seedling lifts her teeny, tiny face, to the giants
that deny her the sunshine's grace.
And asks in a voice so sweet, so shy, "What is the sun?
What is the sky?
Would you let me see it, please, before I shrivel up
and die?"

A mighty tree looks down in disdain, at the little
sprout that cried for rain.
And then shrugs his mighty bough aside and says,
"Just one little look before you're dead."

Then, the sun shines through in a solar flash.
And the rain falls through in a delightful splash.
The shoot shoots high, and her roots down pull.
And her own little leaves begin to unfold.

Her hardening wood squeaks in delight.
She wouldn't rot and die, but she will have to fight.
And reach out for more of the sun's stray light.
And gather every drop of rain that comes.
For she knows she will live to find
her own place in the sun.

Kirsten Brawn-Good

Because My Father Loved Me

My father was an atheist

I walked through the tall iron gates
and below the low-hung boughs
The fragrant, fresh-cut grass was
sprinkled with sparrows

I heard the angels whisper oh
so clearly on the wind
They said he smiled bright light
when they saw his soul ascend

It was a smile of joy of finding
the love gathered all around
A welcoming embracement as
the great love light came down

I feel comfort now in knowing
he felt no trauma felt no shame
And that as he entered eternity
he felt pleasure instead of pain

I hope he didn't turn his back to see
me weep at his ascendancy
It'd make his new world seem less sublime
to know his gain meant my decline

Because my father loved me

I felt it when his eyes lit up
When I followed in his stride
And when I did something strong
And good, he'd puff all full of pride

He taught me those important things
that a man will teach his son
When to be strong and when to fight
and how to treat the lovely ones

My father, thou art in heaven, there is
no place else that you would go
I feel no fear now you have traveled
the eternal bright-lit road

And the angels will continue to
whisper of you on the wind
And I know your soul will be there
when it's my turn to ascend

Kirsten Brawn-Good

The Sacrifice of Isaac

Genesis, Chapter 22:1–18
Excerpt taken from my book The Ostrich Chronicle

It was a particularly orange moon. Harvest in the
cooling month.

His bellicose beams sought foe sought fight. A young
ostrich stuck her head in the ground.

Unlike the bison, so limelight accustomed.

The sound of a father's voice, low boom, insidious.

An ancestral bellow. A template, a calling. Temptation
in a compromising promise.

Oh, illusory adieu.

Like Jesus' mission to gather strays, Sin[1] hunted.

The god, Sin, wanted to take his most loved from him.

With heirs as vast in numbers as stars in the heavens,
Abraham was lured.

"Take your son to the region of Moriah.

Though you be without my crescent horns,[2] set him
afire".

The leather sheath on Abraham's leg skewed.

Torquing about the inlay of lapis lazuli.

Abraham placed the pyre's wood
on little Isaac's back.

The silver resting inside twisted in discomfort.

"Father?" he asked beneath the weight,

---

[1] Sin was a Moon god in the Levant.

[2] Crescent-shaped horns were often present at the altars to Levant gods which includes
both Sin and Yahweh.

"Where is the lamb we're to sacrifice?"

Sin smiled, cajoling, his jaundiced eye poisoning.

"Burning flesh, an aroma pleasing to the LORD,

Burning flesh an aroma pleasing to the LORD,

Burning flesh, an aroma pleasing to the LORD."

Abraham murmured to himself.

Feathered wings flapped in Abraham's chest but were hindered by the thicket.

They remained unfelt.

The silly and defiant curls that bounced raucously on Isaac's head.

Though they caught Abraham's eye.

They remained unseen.

The wind lifted them higher, they screamed their innocence louder than Isaac's guiltless, trusting gait.

Abraham's lips pressed thin, his eyes glistened.

The patter of strong boy's steps transcended his death and echoed in his ears until his ever after.

And his soul dissuaded with a repugnant hiss.

Though they caught Abraham's ear
They remained unheard.

He dismissed the rustle from beyond the thatch, the moving twigs the urgent lows.

"Fathers burn so Sin can eat. If I'd have been born first they'd have sacrificed me[3]".

He justified.

A quiet death, a sliced neck, a bloody rivulet.

---

[3] In some New Guinea tribes, old people are knifed in their back to kill the weak persons in the tribe. It is done by their children who know it will be done to themselves by their own children. It's the custom.

Small bones falling, roasted muscle and flesh.

Like a dog that became again puppy, and pees where
he shouldn't.

In Haran, Abraham had sacrificed other children like this.

Objectivity must slay when subjectivity sleeps.

It must not awaken else trespass the goal.

Love must be conquered by fear, by ambition.

An apple for the teacher if you believe the teacher's present.

Tears undeserved, they remained unshed.

He bound the boy.

Braver than brave, he lay quiet on the altar.

Anatolian silver sharp and deadly,
accustomed to the compassionate slice.

Cosmic conjuncture, not entirely otiose; it
intervened.

Sin couldn't restrain it further.

A ram emerged, stuck, struggling.

A boar ran off, a myrtle tree blossomed.

The ostrich lifted its head and discovered.

Flesh in its claws and, finally, blood on its feathers.

Leaving some Friends at an Early Hour

Recited at my brother David's Memorial

Music was always my best friend, the cohesion in my existence.
From the time I was little, I wouldn't be without my radio.
Music put me to sleep.
She was my most constant and considerate lover.
I love her, so why, sweet lord, must I leave so soon?

I had other friends, too.
My heart poured out for the down and out.
I volunteered my generosity.
Everyone knows, who knows me knows, that to charities, my energy
flowed freely.
I had always a gift for those friends I knew on the street.
Sometimes I gave them a place to sleep.
If I'd been paid for charity, I needn't have spent life begging on my
hands and knees for money.
But it was worth it all.
So why, sweet lord, must I leave so soon?

Then, I had my cheerful companions.
Darlene and Vickie, to name a few of them.
They loved me.
And in their company I understood happiness without alcohol's
assistance.
Then, there were my bridge friends.
You know who you are.
Unfortunately for my health, you guys made stimulants just way too
good a time.

The comradeship and laughs and playing cards.
Oh god. We had fun.
I loved our friendship.

Did I say I love You?
That's okay, I'll say it again. I love you.
So why, sweet lord, must I leave so soon?

Then, of course, there was the team of friends that floated on my waters.
Some found the stream and moved on.
And others bobbed among me.
Ready to be bumped into and enjoyed with banter.

Like Paul, and Leslie and Geri, and Gary, and Mark, and Detloff.
And Brian and Barry, and Bill and Phil, Vincent, Michael and on and on and on and on.

I adored the social, but I made way too many phone calls.
I told Kirsten I wanted to apologize for the phone calls.
I hope now maybe she'll do it for me.
Oh, why, sweet lord, must I leave so soon?

My family: Gayle, Mom, Larry and Kirsten.
I love you all.
But I never felt you loved me back as much.
I strove to be just like you guys.
So self-sufficient and respectable.
I know you tried your best to make me feel good about myself.
You were always kind.
But I never felt particularly good about myself inside.

It was my wildest fantasy to be a prodigal son.
To become the strength for everyone.
The man you could lean upon.
It was unfortunate for me that you were all quite strong enough, thank you, and didn't require my charities:
A place to sleep, a dollar on the street, a microwave, a repaired TV.
Oh man, I think that if I could stay just a little longer,
I might have been successful.
Oh, why, sweet lord, must I leave so soon?

Friends, my memories are friends.
Of building forts in the endowment lands.[4]
Of diving for abalone and, visiting Victoria and seeing cousins.
Of babysitting my little sisters, and making them popcorn in a pan.
And cooking Chinese food for everyone at the Brawn farm. And giving
the sisters gifts of Charlie the dog, of hippy bags, of Eastern philosophy,
of Janis Joplin biographies
and all sorts of things.
And driving the bus on vacations.
And having my buddies over to shoot pool in the basement,
And...

... There are sad memories too, which I can now leave behind.
The loss of wonderful friends, who had to leave early like me.
Only more lonely, and more pitifully alienated from their homes and
families than I was.

I hear the music now.
Not the same tunes I had been listening to earlier.
This music is ethereal.
She's more beautiful and compassionate than anything I have ever heard
except maybe Marta's voice.
But in the end, Marta was just a friend.
And this music, this music is pure love.
And she's clinging to me.

I have to leave now, and she's joining me.
Not just joining me.
But is entwined in my soul's transcendence.
She won't let me leave here without her.
Pure love, compassionate love, she's putting me to sleep.

Did I say I've always gone to sleep with music?
And I have.
But rarely have I ever gone to sleep with so much love.

---

[4] Which is now Pacific Spirit Park

Memory of Aunty Dorothy

Her floorboards squeak
to remind them of her pretty little atheist feet

For years, she did walk her halls
and so then the walls do anguish

As they recognize that they would no more see
her tininess chip religion
as she would debate with him, in earnest

And woebegone are the furniture who cry out for
their truant

Remembering well how wide her table set
And her weight upon her cushion

It's all and all and all you know different than
religions so often suggest

That thou must worship their temple or else

Be damned 'cause absent from the light
of God's eternal lovingness

It's not though how it is, you see, the
truth is that they don't tell

Is that, after having died, she's having
a heavenly everlasting time

And if it is God that is in her absence, if it is God
that is without her spirit, if it is God that is without her joy
if it is God without her chuckle, wit and her sweet face
if it is God without her empathy, generosity and love,
it is God that sits in hell

Good-bye to a Sweet Atheist

Good without God, she did epitomize this virtue

Was friendly to the humblest that would
knock upon her door

She would invite them in, and pour
a friendly cup of coffee

"In good we trust," she always said, "humans
have a strong capacity for kindness

To harbour a wonderful continence and
distribute it out to the poorest."

"I am a leaf," I recall her saying, "all things
die and change their properties."

A buttercup absorbs buttercup, without
awareness of the former

"It is not religion that brought us peace
and healing here," she said

"But understanding through deep and impartial
observation and putting it into government

To be distributed, through compassion
and reason amongst the inhabitants."

She did believe her happiness was wrought by
man and carved by joy among her children

This is where her sunlight and spirit were

"Yes, I am a leaf," she said, "and I am prepared for
such a long and darkened sleep

In harmony with oblivion and
the easement of the mind."

"Come, join our congregation," they said
"Not me," said she

Said she'd pass the night in pleasure
chatting around the campfire

The licks of flame eating its shards
of air, and singing songs

The breeze of the lake, and the shore's warm sand

God may have wailed at her to believe
but she could not, could not, could not
God, should he exist, in his error, then
did create a something that could not believe in him

A being that held stout conviction as to the equality of
humans, a strong drive to protect the stranger. And a
solid confidence in the human capacity to love

Dorothy was a thing of beauty. God knows, to
contemplate upon her is a joy forever

Moon Fell

Moon fell in medley at their feet,
lit broad pastures among the sheep.

Legions baa-ahed beyond the lawn,
beyond the spot Moon fell on.

Shards fell through the fumbling fount,
slipped 'tween the cleaves, 'tween the trout.

Shoals bubbled past into abyss,
beyond the spills where moonlight kissed.

It glid down the cliffs, tumbled in shambles,
displaying valley with lune-lit gravel.

It shed its frock, though, swished up the dip,
to hide in umbrage among dark side gneiss.

Moon fell, Moon fell, Moon fell.

Baroque and multi-fractured.
Amorphous conduit of mythological raptures.

But science's dawn doused her mystical with reason waxing.
Moonwort's racemes renamed themselves Honesty.

Suddenly, goddess not revered, Moon fell.
Oh, solo languorous, orange swell.
All had followed what now scientific mouths repelled.

Vacant crucible. Lips not toasted.
Night ceased its fervent howls.
Chapel barren, left disappointed.
Veil unstripped – Oh, child unwanted.

Pedestal crashed beneath her glitter.
Now lesser of a common sister.
Her waning face a mere light dimmer.
Sure, she affects the tides, so what?
Perhaps without her, Earth's oceans be more temperate.

Once star of stars, magic mother, contemporary of the sun.
Now blemished, no demolished, by acts of facts, reality and
reason.

Supple, soft cell, voluptuous.
Was a dancer throned beyond her eminence, yes!

Suddenly was no manipulative prowl-ess
No doctor presiding on the fullness.

No power provider of the undeserved.
Cried not when Sol shone upon another's facade.

Not chased by Hati or Diana famed.
Lady of wild things did not Niobe's children slay.

Nor turn her into stone and stream.
Endymion was not hostage of, as Cynthia or Selene.

Nor sheltered all of Earth's broken and forgotten things.
Poor sweet flamboyance, fabrication cloaked.

For millennia, framed lucid, fantastic in the minds of all of us.
Unfortunately, most everything she was, she actually was not.
Thus, that's why thought now ran from her lightened touch.

Her deportment lulled gibbous, in such low self-esteem.
She thought even her husband, tried to shake her off of his
sunbeam.
So, one final time, she had waxed and waned.
Jack and Jill did not arise.

Unshed tears dammed each un-dial.
Till dusty basins hid opaqued.

Till attractive power forfeited their magnetic pulls.
Gentle Giant, now ebony draped, had smothered to
extinguishment.

Now, meteors bypassed her veiled glades.
Despite their consanguinity, Earth, sibling,
not contrite. Nay, not ashamed.

Moon fell, Moon fell, Moon fell, to blackness.

Left diminutive stars to speckle the evening sky.
Moon had blacked out. Apparent suicide.

Thus, ravens spanned on Eros' quests.
And Earth scorned Kama's serenade.
Cold replacement wooed instead.

For poltroons filled the romantic field.
Coagulated ink in the philter vial.
Jet substitute for a lunar tress.
But wars were fought by those dark smit.
Aphrodisiac's coffin yawned transgressed.
Obsidian swathed the child's crib.
No bright fingers 'tween familiar boughs.
Angry nightingales tucked in lullabies.
All broken 'neath Moon's absence.
Through Moon's long waited dawn.

Animals ebbed as the shade marched on.

Trout forgot to copulate.
Sheep's woolens thin, broke with frailty.
Seeds sown remained unawaked.
Her Honesty lost its verdant leaves.
Pruning created barren trees.
Which fell with a gentle push.
As their fluids flowed to non-existence.
And the minds of all animals and men, became dull.
Emanations not wild eccentric as on the full.
But weak, laborious, baleful.

The dark nights depressed. Sank all in great intensity.
Overburdened like the manic with her psychosis deep.
Beneath, in Earth's garden, however, a teeny forget-me-not
decided to churn and fan Moon's remembrance.

Remembered everything, but refused to lure the
victims, in the way the victims had lured their victims.
One flower's influence into a greater something was all it took
to fill the fields. The growing fields of forget-me-not hue.

Moon, though remaining absent to the sight, was now, in lore,
and in the deep memories of men, was suddenly…
Was suddenly new, and improved!

Moonwort's spheres decided to grow anew.
The eyes of reason were filtered through.
Suddenly, again, historically speaking -
the night sky's black Moon hadn't really been just the moon.

As an alternative fact of history,
man's imaginings of the Moon became bigger, broader, and more
dazzling.

Sorceress, enchantress, more bosom and refined.

Adoration traced her darkened vacancy across each
evening sky.
Temples arose, stuff congregated to where beams
would've landed if moonlight still fell in the night
as if it were enchanted.

The rumination and uproar and mystical reconstruction
were so complete.
It culminated in interplanetary disfunction.

Not only man, but place and thing granted mystery
a position most omnipotent.

The phantom lorded above the king.
Moon above the Babylonian Sun.

Suddenly, the forget-me-not spiraled
out of control into the world.
To places where Moon would've lit.

Till its yellow dot on blue painted the entire planet.
Like maniacs they were, the entire planet.

Well, Moon was listening, and she heard Earth speak.
Laughed at the view of forget-me-not blue.
Then, after having become a realist herself, reminisced
the days of Apollo and Sputnik.
Cape Canaveral and astronauts.

Remembrance of being useful set her albedo abloom.
She revealed dust flows and ramparts, maria and rills.

Man now crawled around on her lunar field.
Suddenly, even on the dark side, there was nothing
Moon would conceal.

Then full Moon dawned bright.
Phoebe again became full in unobscured sunlight.
The world stood stunned; grass fell from cow mouths.
Hydro fell in price.

The temples fell, too, but still, the moonwort blossomed.
The fish and the animals stood where her moonbeams
would touch them.

Moon fell, Moon fell, Moon fell.

The forget-me-nots cheered, besieged by her dew.
Their task had been won.
Suddenly, the Moon was just the Moon.

Oh, but what a moon it is!

Kirsten Brawn-Good

Eulogy on a Skunk that Died in the Yard

It was 2 days ago you filled my yard
And nostrils with your stinging garlic clove
Like stuck up my nose
Till then
I did not know how articulate odor's rampage
How precisely targeted to offend
For till then
Skunk came through my bedroom window on the
breath of the evening breeze
An odor akin
To the offence of the day's dimmer light
The less need to strain at the expense of sight
Merely the vague musk to the bright fragrance
of the sweet pea
With the marsh quite far away
And you there alarmed by a coyote
With an open mind, and at long range, I did
manage to tolerate your company occasionally

At a distance, you reminded me of the skunk cabbage
in the forest's bog
Or the pot my neighbour is smoking in his garage
Created an energy – an edge, a mere vibrato to the world
Of a land, I ought to stroll
On my list of could dos but won't
In event, I meet a bear
See, I do not take risks
I enjoy bears on TV, but
I do not walk through the thicket perchance to offend a
viper's nest
But some do
Those who find the designated trail too dull
The "don't feed the bears" signs – too cautious

Some climb frozen waterfalls to provoke death. Simple
The video games insufficient for providing an adrenaline rush
And I do not blame you, skunk, for spraying them
for ruining your bed, necessarily
But why me?

What did I do that persuaded you to camp in my garden
Like a terrorist bomb in the London underground?
Me, a peaceful entity, was considering a pellet gun
Why should I allow an obstinate little shit disturb
my meditation?
Evict me from my outside amusements?
And the peace of the billions that can live in harmony?
I tiptoed by your bed, for fear of you waking
Yes, I feared my yard!
Where all had always been quite pretty and peaceful
Or full of rumpus and playful

Unbeknownst to you, I was so nauseated by your
poison
I locked my door and hid out in my basement
Could only peer out my window at the dew on the
daisy
For a fistful of herbs – my desire ached like crazy
The garden bench, miserable, unusable, empty
And envisioned an awful life because of your
explosions

And wondered
What would I do if you
Didn't finally leave me alone?
If you
Did not return to your jungle?
How many skunks I'd subdue if you decided to
invite like loaded uncles?

Kirsten Brawn-Good

And home beside my beans, and beneath my
tomatoes?
If you outed me from my yard
Couldn't have a picnic
Where your striped back curls?

Move…scat…. I tapped on my window
Go away…. leave me alone….
I did not want to hurt you, you who're so adorable
That is when I do not recall the garlic that you shoved up my nose
For, sometimes it is easily forgotten how horrible the
battlefield

Go where your odor will not harm me or any of my neighbours
Go back to the bog, to your home among the Douglas firs
Go where ones are – that are accustomed to your mortars
Hopefully, they won't bomb back and perpetuate your fear
For their garden's been forgotten
Go…. where ones are that are always afraid
Have become used to it that way, so it is blasé
Where reality is the play –
And the death scenes are real
And the rooms of morality are shut by doors of sheer terror
And the escape route of indignity is abhorred and too
infrequently used
You have cause, I understand. But still…
They birth there and die there. – Perhaps forever

The skunk did not move… just lay so snug
It had been 12 hours, and his tail hadn't budged
Oh my God! He's dead, I said
I felt sick, and I felt sad at the loss of his cute eyes
and shuffle
And then, with sad heart, nose plug and a shovel
We ventured the journey pushing plastic wheelbarrow

Digging his very stinky cadaver beneath the floor
of the jungle

Bye-bye, little skunk
So sorry you got scared, and got hit by a car, and that I got mad
Wish you could have gone back to where you were prized
Despite the closed doors and the fear in the rooms
Wish you could have gone back before morning dew
To where they would hopefully just leave you alone
So sorry you died

I wish you could have withdrawn rather than demise
in my garden
However, if you'd lingered – my garden'd be buggered
And I wouldn't have known what to do
My children'd be born in the gloom
Without doors to the pretty outside
I'd have just sat here and cried, then died
And my children'd be born with straight mouths
on their faces
Never entertained, never allowed into the joy of life
But by then, they'd have not minded it too much
Fear can sustain the fight
So sorry you died

Kirsten Brawn-Good

The Dismantling of Vang Church

My family's Church in Norway
Excerpt taken from my book **The Ostrich Chronicle**

It had been said that a fairy built Vang's church of St Tomas[5]

With magic imbued her whimsy bells

Her tines had peeled ethereal, an invitation for angels to come and dwell

Ancient fairy fingered splinters and angel wing dust drew ill to her timbers

Drew the devil to his steeple

As well

Perchance then would hear her out

Let the fundamentalist nap awhile

Like bait, St Tomas waited on God's hook

Now

Since there were beetles propagating beneath heavy bluebell blooms

They spoke mere warning and not forbiddance

Kin, pagan thought, so not for her

And Tyr[6] honed his iron weapon

And the infections eagerly pilgrimed to her door

To spite the exorcists

To be cleansed by beautiful thoughts[7]

For since her airy inset

Inside the oak circle and fairy wand grass

---

[5] This poem combines elements of two churches in the district of Vang, (Vang Church, & Church of St. Thomas) built late 1100's.

[6] Nordic God of War

[7] Because people thought the Church was touched by angels and elves, the sick and ill pilgrimed to Vang Church to touch her walls.

Had made her appear amicable enough

Would be unlike David over Goliath

Unlike Daniel's return from the lion pit

They thought – It's true

The church in Vang was a diplomat in reference to

pagan influence

Perhaps because St. Tomas[8] continued in his doubt

Though convinced upon touching Christ's bloodied wounds

Thus, the church remained in a challenge with restraint

As if its Viking warrior fork tongues[9]

Misunderstood Rome and the thrust of Charlemagne

As if the kneelers of Christianized Norway

Were the ones who held knives above the necks

Of her plunderings

Oh, it seemed, the sanctity of her longship masts that

Capital her nave

Had, in part, been saved

For they had quaffed spirits in her courtyard

Near where the maidens retailed leeks and parsley

And by the corners of their eyes

A smile too demur and sweet for meek

---

[8] St. Tomas was one of Christ's disciples. He never believed Christ was the son of God despite the fact he was with him through his 3 years of miracles. Only after the resurrection, and only after Christ showed himself as a spirit, did Tomas believe he was anything special. Thus called "doubting Thomas".

[9] The half columns have Vikings with stuck out forked tongues representing the flow of knowledge and wisdom.

Kirsten Brawn-Good

Was courted a shameful promiscuity[10]

It was as if Vang church hadn't quite come over

As if the pendulum took a break

As if she knew that bad was good

If it would allow the fundamentalists to sleep

Twin authorities sustaining balance

Two dragons were carved to tug a figure-eight[11]

The crushed velvet bed in Bestemore's carved box

Was slept in long enough

"On the right side,[12] Guri[13]," she said, and was pushed through the girl's thick wool cloak

The brooch clutched her cape alive, contented

Nonplused as the dark nap scratched it's tarnished back

For it could roll privileged above her young, breathing chest

---

[10] 'According to F.N. Stagg in reference to the Church St. Tomas "It was reconditioned around 1615... the priest at Vang preached there once a year–on July 2nd... many sought cures for their ailments in the miraculous powers possessed by splinters from its timbers..." A market grew up near the church of St. Tomas because of the July 2nd service. "Horses were traded, races run, heavy drinking indulged in, and many a fight ensued." Markets continued to be held near the church until the 19th century. But because of fighting and general unrest in connection with the market days the church was torn down in 1808. A new church was built on the site in 1971.' http://en.wikipedia.org/wiki/ Vang.

[11] Two-winged dragons tug on a figure eight are found at Vang Church, symbolizing everlasting combat between good and evil.

[12] Viking brooches were placed on the right side of a cloak so that the sword arm could swing free.

[13] If my mom had followed my maternal grandmother's tradition, her first born daughter would have been called Guri, named after the Prillar-Guri legend of Norway. My grandfather did not like the name of Guri, so, in my mom's case, they decided on the name "Guldis", which my mom changed to "Goldis". The Guri of 1612 warned the Norwegians of marauding Scotsmen coming down their valley, killing the countryfolk. In retribution of their acts of violence, after the ambush, the Norwegians slaughtered ~290 Scots, – Only 8 were known to have survived.

Her restless shoulders, near her slender neck

A mere figurehead it seemed, but wasn't

Its eyes reopened

Animate

A partner now of her dominion

Moving with her

Boiled down old silver, from boiled down old silver, from boiled-down old silver

The gift would be hers for awhile then subsequent

Eternal and treasured

A hand-me-down stream

An experienced traveler through societies

Never lost, only put away

Documenter of human ways

Experience

She'd learn of what works

Because she'd learn of what didn't

Lore, touched over and over and over

They moved out to the porch

The wolfsbane bloomed garrison

And secured their picket fence

They were on their way to the ancient church

Beyond, the lake's glassing glistened

Ripples pre-cursed from the abyss

A monster showed its scalely back

The trolls[14] guarding the valley corridor

Tolerated the Vangsmjosorm[15]

But shushed the gorge to quiet

No lur was blown in alarm

It seemed in the spell of silence

Vang glanced lakeward

Perhaps because the wagon men had put scaffolding about her steeple

Had laid the serpent pinnacles down upon the dirt

Had used crowbars to unpin her timbers that were built without iron nails

Had decided to reject the ancient church

Perhaps that was why the silence beckoned them to glance lakeward

The head had breached the surface

Followed by scalloped undulatings

Vangsmjosorm was certainly a spectacular serpent beast

For a moment on the froth he frolicked

Then, returned below the surface of the lake

Hugin and Munin, the ravens of Odin, stood on a limb

Took the whole scene in

And flew off to report the sad and resolute

display of emotions to Odin

They shut the gate behind them

That Norwegian clan of Vang

The wolfsbane eased beneath their hoods

Bluebells gloomed along the lane

---

[14] Mount Grindane and Mount Skudshorn are on the south and north side of Lake Vangsmjosa. Apparently, before they were mountains, they were the trolls: Tindulf Grindo and Langvein Rise. Ancient legend tells us that the indent of Lake Vangsmjosa was created when the troll misplaced his foot in the soft soil. The waters of the lake were added when the troll wrung out his wet sock into it.

[15] The sea serpent that appears during times of change

Landscaped boles of ash and elm saluted the processioning

To the dismantling of St. Tomas[16]

Yes, it was, as such, the day

When the Prussians bought and took

Their ancient, hallowed walls away

[16] On July 28, 1844, Vang Church was reopened in what is now, Poland. It sits in Karkonosze Mountains to be of use to the Lutherans in Czarma Gora near Karpacz Gorny. Apparently, people that are wed in the rebuilt church are more likely to remain happily married than those married in any other Polish church.

Kirsten Brawn-Good

Someone Special Sleeps Beside Me

The snow is deep.

And it's been here for weeks.

And the temperature is stuck where the ocean shores freeze.

Beneath the blanket,

Ears and mouth and eyes are shut, – won't open.

Only thoughts allowed to speak within their safe sanctum.

Where only silence replies, but in such dimly lit eloquence.

About and above the crystals have formed,

And they appear to have homesteaded.

Brick by brick, – like they don't expect – the cold to end soon.

Glacial waxing, that's what this is.

This chill unexpected – at a time when the tulips were promising to bloom.

This could last ten thousand years, – or more.

It may as well be if it lasts for 10 more.

I need to speak to someone about this.

What is, is cold, lifeless, missing.

For Earth, it's worth the wait,

But a silence beneath a blanket wanes life away too soon.

Is this the end of me, this inert, boring propensity?

Will the feelings I have now drive to the moment of my doom?

Thoughts ask themselves.

Will I ever find fulfillment, happiness, a moment of complete connection?

Will someone warm me, and speak to me, laugh and engage with me?

Will my feet ever feel light?

Will there be sunshine in my room?

Wait. Wait.

It seems, that maybe someone joined me in my questions.

So, I seek the source of my psychic rendezvous.

Perhaps I'll find that someone special sleeps beside me.

Someone special sleeps beside me.

Someone special sleeps beside me.

Someone special sleeps beside me.

Feeling snuffed and comatose, too.

Through the Rubble and Falling Stones

Through the rubble and falling stones
Could some come through unscathed?
So many lost and frightening homes
Where hope is far away

Still justness, strength and personal truth
Can prevail in a war with evil
They unlock goodwill and set it loose
Upon the spinning wheel

For deep inside most men's hearts
Is an Eden of love desired
A few strong hands can rip apart
The fat of fear some men inspire

Then, watch the subtle hand of God appear
At life's most desperate moments
It may come and reveal the road more clear
And ease the gnawing torment

For some, it will remove the fear
And bring the lost soul home

1500 BC – Indus Valley Invader

*A tale about how the pale-skinned Indo-Persian
Plain's people may have entered into India.
Excerpt taken from my book* **The Ostrich Chronicle**

In the beginning, the gigantic serpent Vritra, captured the flow of the
East Asian rivers, and held them in her
Only to spite the wants of eastern Pakistan's and northwestern India's
flora, and fauna
Therefore, the beasts unblessed to be born, withered
And vegetation grew shallow roots fed only by dew
But luckily, amongst the thorny bush, the ephedra grew
With its bitter taste and aroma, when crushed with milk made soma
Made copious quantities
Which the god Indra drank to stimulate his strength, his bravery
And he leapt into Vrita's scalely, yawning doorway
Therein her ribs and fields of 49 fortresses, he raced
And he stabbed out her bowels and freed up the rivers she choked from
the Himalayas
And then flowed the Ganges, the Indus and the Sarasvati
And then, as the waters poured forth, the landscape became lush, and
animals flourished
And man sowed wheat and barley, and held cows and chickens, and
domesticated them
By the shore of the mighty Sarasvati, they raised their families
First by mud and straw
And then, as forthcoming generations found dependable nourishment
By brick masonry
2000 years is a long time for an advanced society to thrive
From commencement to demise
Although some, as the one on the Yellow River and the North China
plain
From 1500 BC to today, have reigned

But I'm talking here about the Harappans who from 3500 BCE, and perhaps earlier
Lived by the waterways which flowed into the
Arabian Ocean
Fishing by the shores and trading with far-off nations
In time, their sundried bricks built street after street after street of ordered dun
Exact as like the web of an arachnid
House after house, town after town
Each sect same as the next
Provided civilized living for everyone
For one million square kilometers
Each brick alike and perfect rock brick after kiln-fired block

Inside the sanctuary, the sage persuaded the engineers to construct this building here exactly like that building there
"We are socialists, you see, we will not have anyone unbathed or starving here, nor will we have our kin living among effluent."
Still, religion ruled too
As religion ruled ubiquitously everywhere
Upon the priest's dais, lotused the stern 'Lord of Beasts'
A lording proto-Shiva, a Pashupati
Who, it was surmised, had populated the world with life
Surrounded by 5 animals
Elephant, rhino, tiger, antelope and buffalo

From his temple from where the humanist derived his strict political power over the tradesmen
Giving equalitarian civic living the same importance as the pharaoh for his pyramid
As Nebuchadnezzar for his armies, as tunnels are to Hamas and so many leaders that were arrogant and wanted to prove and hold their power have done for their own pet monuments that do not help their constituents
The Indus' governments seemed to value peace with their neighbour
Perhaps they saw that the distant nations were inclined to war

And this inclined the Harrapan of the Indus and Saravati to remain
aloof in their own homes across the Arabian Sea
To not engage with Babylonians any more than must be
Like a Canadian to an American, perhaps, I say, it's mere suggestion
When it comes to the arms and deadly ammunition
The Indus Valley proved people were safer without weapons
"We are scared and won't touch them," was said
So, despite the trade that went on, the vast communities of the Harrapan
remained quite distinctive and private
And despite their wide national borders, seemingly
pacific
The sage ruled with a rigid backhand for the welfare of the common man
And the walls rose, and rose for all, and not just for the exclusive
And the Hindu cow that wanders the street and eats the clover
Has no concept of what it is like to be forced to wear a niqab or be
murdered by her father
And walk behind a man, into a meat processing plant

To fill the stomachs of the thriving, dispersed peoples arose the granaries
And though they all still whined, everyone was cool
For there were public baths and pools
And each home had its own toilet which led to covered drains outside
And underground down the street out of town
Drains that gurgled to the accompaniment
The mantra repeats
Counted off on polished faience beads into the main
And, perhaps, letters from beloved were delivered by Indus script on
palm leaves
The urban streets were festooned with terracotta pots
Trailing fertility from their wombs
The men wore dhotis
Cinnabar patted the ladies' cheeks
And artisans drew art for art sake
They drew sleek vase and cast dancing girls adorned in girdles and
anklets, bangles and earrings
And into clothes whirled the spindles

Made of cottons and wool
In the evening, lanterns fueled by ghee
Lit the meanderings down pathways
And inside taverns bustled in the business of bhang beer and butter-fried
chapattis

Occasionally, a Indo-European wanderer would arrive at the pub with
his horse, his cattle, and his woman from out upon the steppe and
they'd invite them in for a beer
They'd hear of his religion
They'd see he'd have a spear
"It's for killing boars, of course, you can't ever be too safe
By the way, where's your knife?"
"Well, we're pretty safe in town here, we don't need knives."
The Harappan replied warily, and had wished he'd lied
"Where's the nearest tree? I gotta pee."
"We don't void outside unless we're out in the fields, but there's a toilet
in the back of the bar."
And while in there pissing away, they'd hear him sing his loud epic
poetry describing the pursuits of those with imperishable fame
And the Harappans did groan civilly over the audacity of the man as the
people lined up at the door to go
They should have been forewarned, for when he finally opened the door
They saw he'd left an enormous puddle on the floor

They had everything, they did everything
Almost everything was perfect
But unbeknownst to them, was the waiting guile of Vritra's cousin
Who lurked beneath the Earth
And roared in a seismic shift
In unending appetite, the ground gaped wide
And like Sita, the wife of Rama, oh so much loved had, nevertheless
been sucked down by a fissure in the Earth
The Sarasvati in 1800 BC
Except for a remnant rill that, like a woman's fragrance may linger on
the sheets after her departure

The Sarasvati tumbled down beneath the ground
To be sucked up by the Indus and Yamuna Rivers

The Sarasvati River dried
And then, beginning at the edges of paradise
The desert suddenly and irrevocably began to rise
For the monsoons, which would annually revitalize its life
Discontinued
The fragrant remnant prolonged Harappa's breath for another 400 years
Long enough for her hair to become entirely unkempt
Her skin sagged, until her flame became entirely extinguished
The brick uneven
And their exterior walls smelling like poop and urine
And the inhabitants of 1700 years of building upon its ancestors
Had to leave its manor and pack its electric car for an extended sojourn
To the Ganges
To find a comparable life and to plant new earth
Upon seeing the vehicle being loaded out front and contented with the
weeds of the desert scape
The Indo-European plainsmen out on the steppe rubbed their hands
With glee
Wanting to be gentle on the kind folks, penetrated the lands
Gent-ill-lee
They, accustomed to the scarcity of plains life, picked the thinning bones
For a while, contentedly
Of where the poplar, cypress, oak, jasmine, lilac and rose had grown
Like America, not good at infrastructure maintenance
(or safe streets) their goats ate the gardens
Drainage system broke, the toilets closed

By the Sands of Jericho

Down by, the sands of Jericho
You were testing your
Seismic beach alarm
Hurricanes slash
Tidal waves bomb
Volcanoes blast the ash
So many lovely people, lay in the mud to die
Why'd you come to bother me?
I want happiness on my mind
Hydrangea, you heartless, boastful bastard
Hydrangea, the blue and pink and purple turn to brown

Down by, the sands of Jericho
You were framing your
Triple pane windows
Raised oceans drown
Parched farmlands starve
A bombs thrill to kill
So many lovely people lay in the dust to die
Why'd you come to bother me?
I want happiness on my mind
Hydrangea, you heartless, boastful bastard
Hydrangea, the blue and pink and purple turn to brown
Down by the sands of Jericho
You were testing your
Diplomatic skills

Enderlee

Do you remember me?
Do you remember me from Enderlee?

From nearby, the old and drooping cedar tree
Where the cougar, wolf and bear

Would comb and plume their
Knotted untrimmed nature

Where her fawn upon the lawn

Would nibble tea of fiddlehead and
Queen Anne's lace bouquet

Do you remember me?
From near the apple tree?

Where we all played amidst our granny's garden?

Do you remember me?
Do you remember me from Enderlee?

From aside the vast and gentle mother sea
Where eagle's shadow falls

On moss and lichen dappled rocky ledge
Only to swoop upon the picnic ground

Of oyster shells near fiddlehead
And pennywort bouquet

Do you remember me?
From near the apple tree?

Where we all played amidst our granny's garden?

Fraser Canyon

Driving down, down, down the lovely Fraser Canyon
Where misfortunes were found
Looking up its rocky bank, it's dark until the sunshine
Which glows upon the cloud
Shades fall from the ancient craggy outcrops
Then, on the east or on the west
I gotta hear the railroad
Buried beside the valley walls
I gotta hear the goldrush
Cemeteries past her Hope
I gotta see the salmon run
I gotta do, I really love her, she's gotta know
Looking back, back, back, beyond her recent past
Where natives awed her with their love
Looking back to when, her gods were much more kindly than
To the ravagements of man
Shades rise from the ancient, damaged outcrop
Her enchantment radiates
I gotta hear the railroad

The Yale

After you tie your horse, leave your taxi
You gotta pass the serpent at the doorway
A pilot, a welder and a salesman
Line up at the board, chalking pool cues
Beer spilt on tile
A woman danced to the blues
And they swilled around inside
She escaped the fire
Quetzalcoatl[17] had swallowed his tail
She's been here a thousand years
A thousand more await the Yale

Speaking from the dirt of their common grave
A wagon drew up full of stories
My grandpa, a native and a negroid man
Chat along the wall quaffing Kokanee
Guitar strings moaned
The Eddy played the blues
And they swayed around inside

---

[17] The King Eddie blues bar in Calgary, Alberta was demolished. I loved that place and held many memories

Vancouver

Where tall blue North Shore Mountains
Nestle with the sea
In salty breeze
Where river arms – where harbour heart
Will never leave
She twinkles – into racemes of city light
Into a carpet – of luminescent bloom
She's a linguist in an international hue
Sycamore and cherry tree
Hold hands – down the avenue
Rain and sun, they spill to blossom
Rain and sun, they spill to blossom
Vancouver's sweet flower garden
Her rainbow –
So beautiful

Where Pacific Ocean let her ebb and flow
Stroke his sandy toes
Let her inlet arms – wrap Stanley Park
Just won't let go
For she walks – in the supernatural
A rhythm – woven by native yarn
A symphony of bliss upon her shore
Purple plum and chestnut tree
Their leaves – mingle in the yard
Rain and sun, they spill to blossom
Rain and sun, they spill to blossom
Vancouver's sweet flower garden
Her rainbow –
So beautiful

I Made a Mistake

I made a mistake
And I'm so sorry!
I didn't cut my hair
So I don't look properly austere
In fact, I look like a slut, tut tut
I haven't been altruistic enough
I haven't been outgoing
I haven't done anything substantial
I sleep too much
I sit on my couch as if I'm handicapped
and therefore have no choice ·
I don't go out and actually shake hands
I got lazy
I'm an error machine
Despite God in my face stands
I'm not righteous enough
I am myself, and I don't want to make that offence
With God and guardians so closely by
I ought to do big, good things
Instead, I just slump in my dump
Content in my den
As life rolls over and life rolls in
I know that there is potential for magic here
And I don't open its conduit
I'm shameful, to have so much power and
not utilize it
I must go out and water the garden
I am oh so sorry if I have disappointed

God and everyone
Please, God, set me right
Instill in me the braveries to fly to Washington, DC
And park outside the white house
I should paint a big sign
And dance unreservedly
It worked for Warner Brothers, sort of
Oh rats. Forgot. I can't sing or walk, or dance anymore

Butterfly Hunter

About the brother of a close friend

The predator stalked within shade
He was an agent with a useful cover that filled
The net with butterfly flutterings so beautiful
A smile, a dot was stuck
Pins stabbed in, a flattened wing, a dashing offering
For the British Museum
Not ready enough to face a fight
He also snuck about taking pictures of Soviet
installations
Sometimes, in the night
The bugologist did well
Since he lay downwind
For butterflies can smell
In covered face and overalls
And he hung about the milkweed
Enjoying what he was doing
Recording the local's lovely ethnic melodies
In Afghanistan, reading ten thousand penguin books for their information
These wrapped his Vancouver room in insulation
For to here, he carried his books and tapes to safety
Away from Brezhnev
And his KGB
Oh, how he had earmarked his pages
With echoes of London, Beirut, and Uzbekistan
A mathematician, a linguist, a musicologist
He had wisdom of many lifetimes
A spy with a broken heart, a broken bank

He who cradled in love with his butterflies
And the lady of red and black
Was pinned to a board
Had posed with scribbled biologic facts
Became a collection displayed at the British Museum
Till the CIA -thought fit to take
His micro-dotted butterflies away

The Blue Rose

The rats, which began so few and harmless
Lingering beneath cherry trees and spitting out the pits
Filling up their plates with food, and pooping on nine-tenths[18] of it
Disdaining God's benevolence by grabbing Eden's ownership
Never seemed to worry as the abundance began to shrivel in the sun
But honed their violent instincts as the landscape went from lush to desolate

It came as bright light, then silvery white
A cornucopia[19] of transforming radiation
And landed innocently abut the vulnerable roots of Rose
The most regal blossom of Eden
And like those from Thrace, Abydos, and Emessa
Corinth, Cyprus, or the Blackstone of the Kaaba[20]
A heavenly rock is often thought to be a godsent panacea[21]

Lustrous and magnetic, the element had pull
And charged infant Rose roots with the authority to rule
But since authorities must learn it first made her white[22]
But meant her to mature into a bright cobalt[23] blue

---

[18] For every 10 units of resources, rats only require 1 unit yet destroy without purpose, 9 units.

[19] Horn of plenty

[20] Blackstone, a meteorite kissed by every pilgrim to the Kaaba at Mecca. Moslems say that it was white when it fell from heaven, but it turned black because of the sins of mankind.

[21] Healing universal remedy

[22] The white rose symbolizes the pure, innocent and unselfish love of Mother Mary. But not in this poem.

[23] Blue extracted from arsenic and sulfur.

The rose dominated with soft, snowy petals
Atrocious habits, and no self-control
Like a baby without empathy
Surviving in a world of cruelty and complexity
Taking only primal counsel

Her pungent perfume[24] and her round, pristine face
Built a strong whited sepulcher[25]
That allowed the damsel Charlie Moore[26] to feed the Smithfield fires[27]

Being young, and with only soft, harmless thorns
She partook of Mistletoe's[28] undivided protection
A parasite residing in her back yard
A friend of pretended affection

The anus scrounging in her apple tree
Was worth the wroth[29] Rose gave him in trust
Cause an arrow empowered to blacken light,[30]she thought, must have
Strong arms to have killed so much

Although Mistletoe baked fresh berry pies for Rose
It was no kindness or act of redemption
Cause the fruit he kissed with Balder's[31] death
Poisoned with guilt, revenge, and tantrum

---

[24] Originally used in sacrifices to conceal the odor of burning flesh.

[25] A whited sepulcher: hypocrite who conceals wickedness beneath virtue. Sepulcher: a holy cave as where Jesus lay.

[26] An old navy term for anything honest and respectable.

[27] Near the central meat market of London. They had burned Protestants at the stake there.

[28] A parasite especially attracted to apple trees. Mistletoe slew Balder, the Norse God of Light. Once a tree from which the wood of the cross was supposed to be made. Has poisonous berries. Toxic in large doses

[29] Values paid to lord for castle protection.

[30] Mistletoe was made into an arrow to kill the Norse God of Light.

[31] The Beautiful Norse God of Goodness and Light.

An Amalthea's[32] horn brimming with the ashen apples of Sodom[33]

After Mistletoe's influence, and Rose's dominance
Rats next took center stage
Bent to blanket and control the Earth
With the power and politics of their offspring
Three hundred and sixty million every three years[34]
By having
Twelve more every twenty-one days
In sewers and garbage dumps, they fucked and rallied
And traveled on ships carrying baggage with bubonic plague[35]

Despite their high concentration
Despite the lack of wealth for consumption
A rat's a rat, a rat's a rat programmed to waste, instincts for combat
Inherited the righteousness to ten-fold his take in pollution
Condescending of others until they could destroy his ability to steal
From him

Obsessed observe Moon circled Earth
Distraught at the demise of the garden
Disturbed by the Sun's[36] teasing and obnoxious aim
To grab at breasts
As if unawares of the diatribe in Moon's speechlessness
And in a way, only innocent obliviousness can
Sun sought to incinerate femininity's influence

---

[32] The name of the goat that provides the horn of plenty.
[33] May be the "Osher Tree" found near the Dead Sea. Parent of large, perfect, yellow, apple sized fruit often with an ashen interior as a result of insect infiltration. Look yummy, but aren't. Also may be the Solanum Sodom[ae] um, small prickly bush with small yellow fruit means disappointment & disillusionment.
[34] The number of offspring by a pair of rats.
[35] Rats responsible for distributing the flea that carries the plague.
[36] The sun is usually identified with masculine, while the Moon feminine.

Worried then, Moon's infection blossomed
At the sight of the Amazon Queen, Thalestris[37]
Asking Alexander the Great
To impregnate 300 left breasted[38] women
Because of it all, Moon couldn't sleep for months
Round lamp burned with one eye pinned open

Unicorn, her ivory companion[39], accustomed to dancing and prancing
Entertaining Moon's eves on her moonbeams
Sat to nurse her fever
Lapped to damp her brow
Mopped to cool her full, hot, infected swell

On Earth, meanwhile, awaited Rose and Mistletoe
They baited Moon's nurse and tickled his unicorn predispositions[40]
"Rose is an endangered virgin!" wrote the newspapers
Wrote the advertisements
Elaborated the gossip mongers in their legislatures

Oh, Unicorn's urge to protect, is as obstinate
As a fruit fly to wine
And as doomed to swim in its crimson slip
So intoxicated by Rose's need he was
While he vowed Moon his devotion
While loyalty nursed her evolving swoon
Oh, still, though, her lovely steed was so obsessed by Rose was he
Had such longing to cause her to move to safety
Oh, how brave he would be
How his hoof would find firm ground

---

[37] Amazon means "without breast".

[38] Amazon women would remove their right breasts so that they could be superior archers. It was more important to have the draw than the bra. Also, if you don't got it they don't grab it.

[39] The unicorn is a mythological companion of the Moon.

[40] Unicorns are drawn to lying down at the feet of virgins. In fact, virgins are used for unicorn bait.

Kirsten Brawn-Good

How he'd be fast and mighty in the material realm

"Help, help!" Rose shrieked. "Please rescue me!"
Moon, though suspicious of Rose's bleating
Finally understood Unicorn's obsession
And, overcoming her fear of Unicorn's doom
Moon gave him leave to his inclination
"Please, my gentle angel, please, please put not
Yourself in peril."
And a tear rolled down her globose plate
A sad smile, a brave face

With that
On a weakening moonbeam, he quickly slid
To where the fair maiden sweetly bid
That waiting poisoned, plotting violent virgin
And her would be accomplice that Mistletoe

When he arrived, he first tested the pie
And with arsenic it was liberally poisoned
So his horn spilt a rich hemoglobin[41]
Although he could slit the belly of an elephant
And he could steal the lion's imperial show[42]
In perfumed repose, Unicorn was betrayed by Rose
And was slaughtered by the fiend Mistletoe

The vision of carnage made Moon want to die
Further, repulsed by the rats fighting to feed
On the corpse of her steed
Exhausted, depleted, she slunk to resign
While Mistletoe poked out his eyes with his thumb
Rose mastered Unicorn's bones on a drum
His sacrifice unnoticed, the violence unabated
At the death of her hope, Moon shut her eye

---

[41] Apparently, unicorn horns can detect poison and when they do, they spill blood.
[42] As per Spenser's 'Faerie Queen'.

Like death. Went black. Gave up

When rays ceased to lead between darkness and light
Then dark became black, and
Light burned harder white
And without the arena for compromise
Extremists were licensed like rats to multiply

And Orgoglio[43] closed his ears
To the poetry of Laurel[44]
The feisty suaviter[45] whispered small and clear
And Aspen[46] trembled in the still of the cold

Besides the masses of rats
The woods were full of other less-consuming animals
Innocents programmed to comply with destiny's deal
As dependents of Eden, they acquired no defenses
Because sunshine spoon-fed them their meals

Harmless and cooperative, they'd take rides with strangers
Laughing and ignorant rolled their tummies into danger
Only when they organized and counted lives did they gather
Too many of them had become some other friend's dinner

When they were young, they danced around Rose
A little bossy, they thought, but she played with them
When Mistletoe arrived with his arrows and bows

---

[43] Arrogant pride. The sin of Satan. In Spenser's 'Faerie Queen', pride was the sin of the Catholic Church. Orgoglio was a hideous giant, as tall as 3 men who represented the tyranny of the church and Rome. His castle home had a plush room containing an altar spilt over with the blood of martyrs.

[44] Ancients felt the laurel communicated the spirit of prophecy and poetry. Placing laurel under one's pillow may provide inspiration.

[45] Gentle manner yet resolute in action.

[46] Due to its shape and construction, the aspen leaf appears to be always trembling. Mythologically, it is said to always tremble because of its shame and horror of being the wood of the cross that Jesus died upon.

They viewed his manipulations with unacquainted trepidation
That's when he poisoned her

Then the world became hot
Tempers flared in time with sunspots
Some herbivores became carnivores and fed
On a spree of tasty, unsuspecting sops[47]

Teeth became scissors, and nails became knives
Like the rats
Mostly, those only with the conscience to conquer
Were destined to survive
And the silly Atlantic salmon laughed unconcerned,
Like an audience from a distance
Despite the fact that rats dive one hundred feet[48]
And would fill his ocean with garbage
America felt indestructible within their retreat
By the distance, it is to their continent
Of course, they had to contend
With their own kinds of domestic violence
But they had till now maintained
A balanced equilibrium in their local environment

With the hostility of Thor[49]
The clouds became dramatic
Global Warming ignited forests to the applause of thunderclaps
Furry victims of nature would run from the fire
And quiver till it dusted down to ash

Conflict and confusion, friends and foes sometimes indistinguishable
They dug their own little shelters from the swelter
As the heat became unbearable

---

[47] A yummy piece of meat for Cerberus the 3 headed dog, to allow passage into the gates of Hades without being molested by his violence.

[48] Rats can dive 100 feet.

[49] Nordic God of thunder and lightning, God of War.

No hospitality accepted lest one became the feast
Eggshells crushed beneath little fleecy rodent feet
Only at night did they venture to forage
Among the flowers and the fruit trees

Fear increased as seclusion and depersonalization
Had reduced every individual's pelt
To a commodity of public consumption
Then, one night, as they were beginning to feed
They gazed as a gallant stallion[50] danced down
On the rays of a droopy moonbeam
The animals rejoiced and partied
And cajoled their friends from their dens
Even the rats were intrigued by the concept
Of the thrill of battle with a good and worthy opponent

Confident fools, the animals ate their nuts and preserves
And bravely drank from the brook
Reliving their good times, they lost their fears and controls
Till they viewed the slaying of their savior[51] by their enemy, Mistletoe

They slumped as their perception of paradise fled
The rats yawned and turned their backs in contempt
At ease again
In the surety and strength of their proliferating governments
Light left the night as Unicorn was shredded
Without illumination, the other animals were unable to find feed
And they became easy prey if they foraged by day

Gentle creatures gathered together on the beach
To kiss the anchor that had long corroded till it was down to
One small core piece
Through the dampness of man's transgression
Despite its flaking wormholed fabric orange and dusting

---

[50] The unicorn represents Jesus Christ and his horn, the gospel of truth.

[51] An anchor is the Christian sign of hope.

They padded it with revised understandings
Gooped up its crevices, wrapped it in duct-tape
And in a new obsession, mused on their dream

They conspired to seize Unicorn's tusk
Which, when ground and eaten
Would neutralize the poison[52]
Which their bane fertilized Rose with from dawn until dusk

Porcupine was the first volunteer
In a world of vegetarians, he required no armament
But when pork became cuisine, he found his friends were enemies
Thus, to protect his pudgy belly, he developed an arms depot
A tank of the perimeter clubbed-tailed military industrial complex
Nature's enemy obstacle
His defense had grown most adept at daytime offense
A tasty meal beguiled below the quills
Which penetrate intruders with 1001 barbs[53] of flesh-ripping steel
Organ seeker sabers bent on fatal rupture
Rotund stature, cute little eyes, little bit shy
Prepared to strafe and tear the flesh of Mistletoe's stem

Flat-footed mop shuffles, then slow, proud and comfortable
Handsome in black tie with secretions intact
The animals respected the disarming proclivities
Of the intriguing and sophisticated polecat[54]
Once, when the world was kinder, he was an applauded perfumer
An odor ornamentor of the very highest rank
He'd gather fragrant essence and retain them in his fixer
His belly became fat as remuneration for his skank[55]

---

[52] Apparently, ground and eaten, the unicorn tusk can neutralize poison.

[53] Well, actually a thousand barbs, but made the allusion to Salman Rushdie who does 1001 of everything

[54] Another name for skunk.

[55] This is all true. Skunk secretions were used as perfume fixers. The musk, once the odor was removed, would help sustain other fragrances.

Everybody in the forest loved to dapple on his fusions
Feeling debonair and suave
They'd drink martinis in the grass
He worked beneath his sign of bleached stripes on ebon
And became a tourist attraction in the little Ville de Grasse[56]
But then times became less kind and he adapted to the danger
He was signed too well to hide, so he acquired a strong defensive tactic
He found his unique talents made him king of chemical warfare
Foul fumes and burns and blindness
Would skunk a squadron of intruders
Now everyone stayed clear of the pongy little cat

Behind the fatal bomb, behind the poison gas
Squirrel and Chipmunk
Would employ a grayer side of breaking nuts
The others gathered their strengths and their confidence
Resolved to grab the tusk
And destroy the nasty incubus[57]
They prepared to risk their lives if it would bring the world into balance[58]
Ninja masked secret agent[59] set out to scout advantage
With stealth approach he spied upon the apple tree
Wherein Mistletoe resided

He observed an honest postie leave with several parcels
He observed mercenary[60] rats and weasels
Garnished with spears and arsenal
To gauge their temperament they arranged a duck to sit
Thank God he was made of plastic
For it exploded into the fragments before the ground was lit

---

[56] A French town near the Mediterranean famous for its perfumes.
[57] Something that oppresses or discourages. A demon that has sexual intercourse with sleeping women. A demon that causes nightmares.
[58] Balance, an optimum condition. The world is currently unbalanced.
[59] Raccoons
[60] Warriors that slay for pay, not necessarily honour.

Kirsten Brawn-Good

The origin of their misery would not be abducted easily
Alert behind a fortress dripping in poison ivy
But the creatures understood patience
Was like water, the world's most powerful tool[61]
Calmness and forbearance
Was the key to their performance
That would lead to their opponent's downfall
Finally then, less guarded, Mistletoe left his palace
To a clearing in the forest to engage in target practice
The animals were prepared now to sneak up and to abduct
Then question the skinny stick until he told them where to find the tusk

Porcupine would take the hedges that encircled the shooting range
Where Skunk would bravely saunter in and begin the coup de main[62]
Bold adolescent bucks would herd vermin into the pits
Which Gopher had dug with ease and camouflaged in foliage
Mistletoe was usually careful, protected by a very, very large army
But this one time went boldly less protected into the clearing

Here he comes, they signed silently among their unconventional order
Skunk tiptoed in and puffed Mistletoe and the rats with his odor
Then as some grunts weaved through quick to his defense
They were pummeled and felled by Porcupine's shrapnel
Eager deer[63] drove their foes into the holes
Over which elated frowns looked down on them and Mistletoe

The grunts were made helpless
Saint Sebastion[64] offered slim resource
Were taught to die than kiss the emperor's feet

---

[61] Water is the universal solvent.—just takes time.

[62] A blitzkrieg, a strong, sudden attack resulting in a pivotal victory thus resulting in change.

[63] A large, and usually non-contesting herbivore.

[64] Became patron saint of soldiers. In 288 CE in Rome, was a Roman soldier. When he was identified as a Christian, he was strung up and pierced with arrows, as if a pin cushion. Left for dead, he recovered from the attack, but was later beaten to death.

Were taught to kill to avoid Satan on his MTV
No grunt would submit for his own liberation
Rather be told to die than enjoy celebration, till
One made escape and without observation
Slunk back into the fortress to pick up some reinforcements.

Meanwhile, the creatures couldn't jibe and jest and dance around in mirth
To them there was no joy in performing these kinds of dirty work
However, they had no sympathy for the evil that slew their savior
And in grim discussion opined options for his torture
Rack, strappado[65], Procrustes' bed[66], or
Whatever pain that their ethics could muster
They discussed these things carelessly, then deeply for a bit
And decided not to use the methods common with Mistletoe
That poison stick
Of course, Chipmunk and Squirrel were ready and waiting
To do anything not too mean
Still, they feared he may lie to them
Before he'd tell them where to find the unicorn vaccine

"It's in the mail. I've got the postal slips to prove it."
He pulled them out to show them from his muddy walled depression
The animals wanted to deny the facts
But they recalled Raccoon's covert intelligence
"I divided up the remedy and sent it in little packages
And you guys better watch it!
Because I'm being supported with allegiance by every violent highness."
Earth confirmed he was telling the truth
When she shot up sprouting violets[67]

---

[65] Torture, where one is pulled to ceiling and dropped.
[66] Mythological iron bed of torture on which men were made to fit. If too tall, the overhang would be cut off, if too short, would be stretched to fit. Thus, a move to standardize thinking would be to put one on Procrustes bed.
[67] The colour violet represents the love of truth, and the truth of love.

And the faces understood
If the wine got switched at a Borgia mix
The tusk would save the life of Caesar or Lucretia[68]
Just then they heard a noise behind
A rustle and a clamour
Porcupine was speared and squealing
And humbled by rats in total body armor
Who strode about the jailors prepared to fight in unaccustomed honour
For the freedom of their leader

The animals were fluffy, but the animals were not dumb
And though they knew the strength of the Lord
They'd decided not to circumcise their sons[69]
So they saw they were standing on Towton field[70]
They saw Cerberus[71] watching with his frothy tongues
And though the houri[72] were beckoning
And vintage wine pooled about their skirts
They had no worth
To soldiers who preferred the feedback from love
And the occasional sip on earth
And Valhalla[73], it looked tempting
But the animals were not ready for a feast
Until they'd gained the horn and caught and subdued the beast
Despite that, they freed their enemy

---

[68] The Borgias were a powerful Italian family. Pope Alexander VI was a Borgia, and his children, Lucretia and Caesar, would rid themselves of unwanted friends by inviting them over for a glass of poisoned wine.

[69] Apparently, if the sons of Abraham break the covenant by not circumcising their sons, they would be suggesting they have deserted their Lord. Thus perhaps, one may suppose, the Lord would desert them too.

[70] Bloodiest field of warfare during the war of the Roses, the House of Lancaster, represented by a red rose, and the House of York, represented by a white rose.

[71] The 3 headed dog at the entrance to Hades.

[72] Virginal man pleasers of Islamic paradise.

[73] Nordic feast to which brave warriors would be taken to after being slain during warfare.

And performed yoga on the Plains of Abraham[74]

Since they couldn't gain the horn, Wolfe and Montcalm shared a dram
Still Mistletoe remained leery of the formidable furry clan
And so with lecherous diplomacy he tranquilized their whiskey
And they returned into the forest sucking blankies and holding hands

And the rats continued to proliferate, to condescend
To destroy all and to maintain control
And enjoy the profitable alliance with Russia and Iran

So the animals had to devise a very different twist
To balance the harmful innocent
And rescue the crystal[75] she toyed with in her fist

Incantations and mithridate[76], they hoped
Would change her from something awful
So they gathered seventy ingredients
Plus Wall Pennywort[77] and Thistle[78]
"Super cala fragile istic" Mary Poppins sang her song

But Rose refused to take the pill
For Rose would not vote for equal rights
Her geld not donate past her pall
For would not wish her vulnerables exposed to welfare's stingy hand
And who'd deny that without the armour of advantage
Equality's a vicious human race
Besides was without the wisdom required to grace the scythe
Down the uncut path to peace

---

[74] Spot in Quebec City where the British General Wolfe, and the French General Montcalm engaged in battle.

[75] The world

[76] A truth serum

[77] Symbol of honesty, its other name. Also called Moonwort as shaped like the Moon.

[78] Symbol of defense

So Rose was without incline for the goal
Where the entire world is first
So that's why Rose refused to take the pill
Perhaps if they had promised it with sugar
Perhaps if kiss had pledged to blush her tush
Of course the integrity in them couldn't
So instead of swallowing it nicely
Rose let the pill
Drop
Into
Her
Dirt

And so then the bluebirds[79] were directed to sing for her
In the park by her plot
To try and fill her with happiness, love and wonderful thoughts

It failed, for Rose despised their merriment
And Mistletoe enjoyed playing cop
So they were arrested and marched off to prison
Beaten and bruised by the muzzles and handcuffs

And Orgoglio closed his ears
To the poetry of Laurel
The feisty suaviter whispered small[80] and clear
And Aspen trembled in the still of the cold

Oh she was awful, an unbelievably selfish youngster
A baby queen in contra mundum[81], who sucked life from all around her

---

[79] Their presence supposedly brings happiness.
[80] To "sing" small, is to make steady assertion and then apologize.
[81] Meaning, against the world at large.

Akrasia[82] ruled from Berlin[83] to the plains of Armageddon[84]
Oil fires and bone fires[85] tarred the wind
Brethren stained the weapon
Of ones left standing after the onslaught of typhus, plagues and infections
And rats killed rats who wouldn't kill rats
But who would honour the one's that would kill them
And from the vast ocean the great white sharks sang the blues
In humbled acceptance of murder, pollution and annihilation
Thyestean feast[86] with every cup of coffee
Because vengeance was the elite's most favorite entrée
Cassandra[87] gagged on an apple as they sliced flesh from her belly
Egos remained militant toward differing opinions
While senses grew tolerant of a more putrid environment
Which expanded like waves of filth in every nth direction
From the source which was once the site of the Garden of Eden

So she stood above all through the triumph of her pallor
Surrounded by black, godsent Rose could build sacrificial altars
Unending bleakness because her whiteness made her fadeless
In love with the pain, she victimized lovers
That was, until she grew older, and her petals began to change colour
Maybe it's a myth
Maybe the possibility is truthful
Maybe somewhere secret
There grows a rose so beautiful
Coloured blue like lively oceans
Coloured blue like clean skies
Coloured blue like the happiness that returned to sing by her side

---

[82] An enchantress signifying lack of self control. She transformed guys into monsters and kept them captive.
[83] City from which Hitler ruled and ordered the holocaust.
[84] Apparently, the earth's final battle spot where the Lord purges the world of most of man.
[85] Bone fires, meant burning bodies. Word became bonfires.
[86] A feast where human flesh is served. Thyestes was the father who was invited to a feast where the limbs of his two sons were served in a dish.
[87] Prophetess or fortune teller

Kirsten Brawn-Good

Blue feathers whose beaks played ball
With the berries of old Mistletoe
Who was replaced by a trail of wormwood[88]
On where he slithered out to go

Maybe somewhere there's a rose of such a blue colour
Who only strives for peace when she's dealing with others
But who always questions the food that is placed upon her plate
Who knows it's a difficult line between being early or late
Who knows balance is found in a vast world between virtue and sin
Who didn't know any of this
Until the medicine seeped down into her pale rose roots
And her "W" chromosome set in
To concentrate her blood with a pigmented antitoxin[89]

Maybe where Aspen's still
And where Laurel speaks strong and clear
Maybe there's a rose

There stands a rose bush, right in the center of the market square
Because her nice blossoms were always removed, everyone ignored her
But deep within her roots, within her inner sanctum
Beneath the social layers before the congregation
Deep in a cavern, sub rosa[90], where Johann Andrea[91] once roamed
The antidote sparked a little sprite
A cryogenic[92] passenger of the meteorite
I call "W" chromosome

---

[88] Wormwood was said to have grown in the track of the serpent as he fled the Garden of Eden.

[89] Something that reverses a toxic aspect.

[90] Clandestine, deep secret, beneath a bud that is above two rosebuds — not in the roots.

[91] Johann Valentin Andrea (1586–1654). A Lutheran minister, who, through perpetuating a hoax, created the Rosicrucian religion whose disciples still, apparently, await the world to fall into blissful balance.

[92] To be put to long-term sleep through cooling of the body and a slowing of its metabolism.

Now "W" had an amazing periscope
With which he'd eye aloft from every angle every morn
He shook his head as Podsnap[93]
Flailed himself and honed his crown of thorns
And stifled the individuality in others from which
Their personalities were born

And "W" asked – Why? – Why?
When God gives a gift do they return it directly back to sender?
And asked – Why? – Why?
When doors are open for learning, do they just sit and just get stupider?
And asked Why? Why? Why?
Was Rose's blueness considered blasphemous?
And thought maybe a little wrong is sometimes good
If virtues could so obviously hurt you

Oh, it was a potent chromosome, a latent evolution
A tranquilizer of such a caliber it could spark a huge halcyonic[94]
revolution

"W's" vat brimmed with cobalt blue, an explosive, non-aragonic[95] potion
In which Kismet[96] came to skinny dip, like a toast in celebration[97]
As a lion he skimmed dew[98] from the Alchemilla rose[99]
And swept his footprints from behind him[100]
And added diamonds to the liquid 'cause they're only cut by diamonds

---

[93] Pompous self-satisfied man

[94] Halcyon days, days of happiness and prosperity.

[95] Peaceful, (as per Nostradamus) where aragonic, means with violence.

[96] Fate, destiny, fulfillment of destiny.

[97] They once used to put toast in tankards of wine. The toast became the object of the compliment. Apparently, during the reign of Charles II, A fellow took a glass of water from a bath in which a lady lay. When offering the water (liquor) to his friends, one said, forget the wine, but would have the toast.

[98] In alchemist terms, dew dissolves gold.

[99] The rose leaves from which the dew was drawn by alchemists.

[100] Apparently lion tails wipe out footprints so that their presence remains undetectable.

Kirsten Brawn-Good

And he even threw in a spearhead from that Bradamante[101] woman
He tossed in a lovely bezoar[102] from within a departed goat
And tested the fountain with falsehoods
To see if they'd sink or if they'd float[103]
Last, he ladled in some lyddite[104], and angelica[105] and common sorrel[106]
And poured it into barrels, and awaited serendipity[107]
While listening to whispering Laurel

Within the penetralia, he could only dream and think
So on the odd occasion, when he craved some inspiration
He'd touch Rose with ink
What violence would materialize
Upon the new blue bud
They screamed, "Someone must be sinning"

Though her petal placed beneath a tongue could purge the plague[108]
From a daughter or a son
They preferred to bury bodies than engage in an act of love or reason
By having a Covid inoculation
So they'd send out their man from Banbury[109]
Instead to burke[110] her with a trimming

---

[101] A Christian Amazon woman who possessed a spear that unhorsed every knight it struck.

[102] Stone from the stomach or gall bladder of either goats or antelopes. Set as a jewel was believed to be an antidote against poison.

[103] Referring to 'trial by water'. If telling the truth, the person would sink and drown, if lying, he would float and be executed.

[104] High explosive

[105] Herb of the parsley family used in defense against plague and pestilence.

[106] Herb of the buckwheat family representing joy.

[107] Luck found through unexpected accidents.

[108] The vitamin C absorbed by rose petals placed beneath the tongue helped cure victims of the plague.

[109] A Banbury Man was considered to be a Puritan or a bigot. A man from Oxfordshire, known for its puritans.

[110] To smother at birth

And Orgoglio closed his ears
To the poetry of Laurel
A feisty suaviter singing small and clear
And Aspen trembled in the still of the cold

I believe, God gave us the world
To see if we'd grow wiser
But it seems the precious means to growth
Has been dug beyond the fertilizer
For it seems a decline in the environment and the human situation
In too many cases, apparently lies in the hands of heaven
When, in fact it lies in the hands of the ones
Who went to rape and spend them

Cause God has continued to be the default
The violently wielded broom
A benign, absorbent scapegoat
For the rats who've been snipping the buds before they bloom

Else why are religious truths so dumb, like transubstantiation?[111]
And why do they appear to have mostly political and social boundaries
If they're a universal dictation?

Why does God's love too often appear
In so many isolated, fanatical territories?
Where his sweetness is polluted by fear driven stories
Created to prod the cattle into ambitious armies
Killing, always, first for God
When it's really only just for the power and the glory?
It seems the world's ability to balance
Has been leveraged against harmony
Volumes of different agendas have been stacked high
On only one side
Understanding of ourselves

---

[111] The method by which the bread and wine apparently become the body and blood of Christ.

Others
And the Earth has been locked out of position
Steel beams and mortar replace the give and take between
Our sexes, countries and our religions
Heavenly virtues contradict
Because in fact they're only organized schoolyard opinions
Where to gather the most powerful clique of patrons
Is the real competition
Then, Xiphias[112] entered the nighttime sky
Only to visit the orbiting kingdom
"Ours is not to question why," they hymned
And arranged an antediluvian[113] solution
So that even the libertines[114] fettered in bilboes[115] did their best
To slay their only children
The Aspen froze in fear, oblivious to the promise of the feisty suaviter

Now "W" had a feeling that the sitzkrieg[116] was almost done
Cause Moon in urgency had relit to balance the sun
And then he looked to see that suddenly millions
And millions of microscopic buds had begun
They had stored enough energy
For a non-pyrrhic[117] victory
The world was finally ready and required the cobalt blue palladium[118]
And so he uncorked the barrels and the pigment coursed in
To the reservoir waiting behind his syringe
Counted one, two, three and plunged in the pin

It stormed through her roots, and surged up her stem
Radiated through her veins, through the world

---

[112] In medieval times, and right now, it was the name given to a sword shaped comet.
[113] Anything hopelessly outdated, meaning, before the flood.
[114] The most free or liberal thinking of a group.
[115] Sliding fetters, or bars of iron, linking prisoners together.
[116] During a conflict, a period of such quiet, that there appears to be no military activity.
[117] A war won at NOT too high a price.
[118] An object essential to the safety of a community.

And through her blossoms

Because it was natural for Rose to have hue
She orgasmed in pleasure as the antidote pulled through
Every mini bud exploded into beautiful enormous blossoms of blue
The animals danced together
And violets bloomed amongst the broom
And though a rat's a rat a rat, they're very different from the humans
Animals rejoiced as Unicorn arose from new Rose roots
He sped up on a moonbeam to rejoice with the Moon
And that was when her thorns matured to protect her decree
And it was the first time in a long time Canada's salmon felt safe in the sea
And Laurel spoke with love of the victory of peace
And Orgoglio unplugged his ears and became equal with others
And the pruners saw the beauty in their sons and their daughters
And Aspen was still and relaxed as the sword flew from his heaven
And the rock from the stars smiled from the Garden of Eden
Is there such a Rose? I don't know
But Laurel says there's one

Kirsten Brawn-Good

Just a Warning

God was robbed while taking his phenomena to a place of concealment
He was not thieved of love, hope, kindness, fortunately but
Fiends took all the rubbish: money, pride, power
Honor and other various sins
And meant to poison through them

Eternity
Surrounds the sea
And all of God's most important gifts lay in wait for us
These most important things in existence mostly remained within God's
tired ancient cognizance
Unless speech ambitions to his tongue and influences though
To sow love
Explodes upon his yawn
And he naps
And the manipulative, hateful acts of men deploy the filth
As they always have done
To honor killings and mass poisonings
The fascisms of social identification could win unless there are
adjustments
Unless the Jews can live peacefully with the Palestinians
Unless the Russian can live without aggression against the Ukrainian
Unless China can live without controlling Tiawan
Unless Spain can live without warring against the English, what? That's
solved? There is hope then?!
Disloyalty carries a death penalty, upon the common's hymn
After World War Two, Russian soldiers shot returning Russian soldiers
for only Stalin's authoritarian reason

And Donald Trump promises retribution and vengeance against those
that sold out to save their own skin
In that dreadful mix, they are hard baked in fear
Yes, the rubbish sold, spreading schisms through forums

Of religion, communism, fascism, capitalism, Rupert Murdoch, the
NRA, Alex Jones, Steve Bannon, and so on
Unlikely as it sounds, but quite possibly
The misty mushroom cap may win
Falling upon the misinformed on all sides
Those that would have loved but for the mastermind
Who, negligently, replaced the emptied space with sleep and allowed the
fiends to reign
The world
The infected sore
With too few in too much richness
Stealing from the hordes
Of starving religiosity
Not getting from God
What was promised
No, forget that, I don't mean forget that, but forget that
Was the jobbed against the jobless
Was the false sense of worthiness amongst the insecure
Was the buyers against the manufacturers
Was the renters against the owners
Was the preachers against the congregation
Was the living dead against the living
Clearly, something must be done to assist the impoverished!
To bring the loving soul to self-worth
To heal the wounds of the down and out
To reverse religions' adverse potentialities accrued during swings of free
reign
But this healing potion is in God's sleepy hands

God awaits, and his application of love is easily done upon the reaches of
Heaven
However, here is war as the fiends happily manipulate their extremisms
for their maximum benefit
Who said mediocrity was not good?
Who said families should not love their promiscuous wayward aunt?
Who said there could not love be between the Republicans

And the Democrats?

God may be napping, but on closer examination, he didn't leave us
entirely destitute
We don't see it. But there is plenty of love energy that God supplied, but
it is corked
The beatitude between this world's inhabitants,
Between its countries
Between populations
Exists

There may be seven trumpets, but there are also seven angels
And the angels weren't pouring vials of filth, they were pouring a smile.
Vial and smile rhyme, so the words were easily misunderstood
God could wake up and apply devotion further
And amplify his love in his religious discourses
Could espouse affection freely outside the congregation, clean the
wounds
Bring goodwill and happiness
I know God exists, he is very capable
And God knows me
But God did not necessarily plan to do this, it seems
It must be up to us
It is we who must neuter the fiends and to wake God up
But we find this particularly difficult to do
Wake up God, wake up!
Was the leaders, lining up of chilly tents
Far from the fence

All sides, sabotaging themselves
By sabotaging others
For, what they thought was from God
Freedom and sufficiency won't become
By masses electing filthy rich dictators with perpetuity penchants
And with dreams of becoming much richer by allowing corruption by its
oligarchs and sub lieutenants

It was a powder keg
And it blew
And the future and democracy became scattered on the fallout's dusty
floor
To consummate their atomic fate
Manes rising up from the ground they lay on
The ghosts of the competing indoctrinations
Hugged
"There you are! Finally found you! I love you, my lovers, it could have
been good, but unfortunately, we all must now fly to heaven. It would
be nice to have your company on the way, ok?" "Okay! That's a deal!!"
And they flew into the waiting, loving, warm arms of God

Won't You Assist Me in My Slumber

Fern-filtered sunlight filters past the ivy and warms
up my pillow
A summer's breath draws and billows the drape on my windows
Kissing my linens with lavender bloom

Won't you assist me in my slumber?
My bed is cold and lonely, and I yearn your milk
and honey
Sheets draped upon our bodies tied together
in the middle
Don't you know I love you, darling?

Won't you assist me in my chamber?
I can't seem to hook my brassier, and I yearn
your dexterous fingers
Arms wrapped around our centers, kisses leading
us to linger
Don't you know I love you, darling?

Won't you assist me in my life?
I will not find another, and I yearn your
tender comfort
Love holding us together, leading us to somewhere
Don't you know I love you, darling?

Gentle wind moved the curtain
Kissed my room with lavender bloom, turning sleepy
in the garden beneath the hot, hot Sun
Beyond my sill, squirrel clambered and fell, enjoyed
one by toying with the other

Not too serious, but their tails were tall and stopped
to sniff the lavender
I live in the dirt level with all the insects and rodents
I live in a zoo!
And nature is the main attraction
It watches as I reach to water my begonia garden
Its funny how these things flourish in the shade
Don't you know I love you darling?

Kirsten Brawn-Good

For Ein Man Mit Keine Mercy

In Response to John Keats' Poem,
La Belle Dame Sans Mercy

Oh, miserable knight, whom I do love,
you won't long wallow in despair.

There was an honour in my sweet moan
and a reason I left you there.

Do not fret, for the birds will sing again,
forever twice as strong.

And the withered sedge on the drizzled lake
will grow again fast and strong.

Please, I have faith that you will forgive me, sir,
as I was as insecure as many a maid will be.

When she meets a rover who moves her heart,
a man dashing, strong, and free.

I mean, why do you think my eyes were wild?
Why do you think my foot was light?
Why do you think I made such sweet moan?
Because I love you handsome knight!

But you're a man who may take to a kindly maid,
to please him only until he leaves.

Oh, ich wise ein man mit keine mercy.
I do. So, I left you as the one to grieve.

And when they said I had you in my thrall,
I thanked God they spoke true on your last dreaming.

Because without your forsaken and aching heart,
I'd be the one alone and pale and loitering.

So, it was fun to watch you so sad and dreary
as many a beautiful belle bounced by.

The world laughing and dancing around your spot
of gloom you glorified.

As you did moan, my eyes smiled and saw,
you languish endlessly over our every kiss.

Repeat a million times our whispered words,
missing your merciless, long-lost miss.

Oh yes, and my female might enjoyed to realize,
how to bring you, a merry wight, to cry.

How to make the birds cease to sing.
How to barren the cold hillside.

But fear not, my love, for I will come,
I will mop your sopping tears.

For though you have lost your manly freedom fight,
what you will have gained are love full years.

For I pray you have gleaned from your forsaken state,
the terrible drive for mutual harmony.

And that it is a full, warm, and lovely place,
when I feel for you how you feel for me.

And I will sweep up the cobwebs from the elfin grot.
We'll have puffy pillows and candlelight.

And the birds will sing,
and the sedge will flourish on the lake.

Forever, forever, forever, my handsome knight.

Hals House

My mom's boyfriend

His house was comfortable, but he eyed dreamily out the windows
A liberal spirit with a conservative streak
He had the most warm and comforting smile
A disposition built to set at ease
A sensitivity to the souls that surround him
Respectful of the shelters they live in
In conversation, he was a joiner of perspective
Even if not a joiner in the movement
He understood that experience builds your house
Some people build their homes, shut their windows
and then sit by the fire to die
But not him
He would sit beneath the stars with the others and
barter experience
A valuable yielded by time, energy, emotions, history, and life
Thus, he'd listen for listen
Consideration for consideration
We loved Hal
Our homes are full of him
His smile and understanding are nailed to our walls
His warmth has strengthened our foundations
He is alive, and well, and kicking in each of us
We will never forget him

My Waterfalls

I watched the windswept walls
Surround my waterfalls
My hardness left me somewhat recluse
But deep inside, I felt sunshine
Though cold stone, I was geode
Unknown by everyone
For a flying bird dropped me in her turd
Before my words began to blossom
All these feelings I must express
And at the moment also, harness
Bright and also honest, kind and also honest
In love and also honest, reflect God and also honest
Make peace but then to fight on
Of course, I admit I'm a few of these things, but
What kind of tightrope am I on?
What do you want more from me?
The flies are circling around my spot
As I leave a boastful legacy
My intestines are flying everywhere
Seeking more nutrients, I feel inadequate here
I don't like to feel inadequate
I feel inadequate there
I don't like to feel inadequate
My face says I don't, but I do care
I'm frustrated my seed is burst
When I become one, I'll be two again
Maybe it's time to cut my hair
No, express myself instead, they said
I have no ******* control
I have no ******* control
I have no ******* control
Fortunately, I'm wise enough to know
I volunteered to continue to be good, and to have no

******* control
At least the initial choice was mine
If I really needed to be free, I'd leave this life
I'd choose the time, I'd choose the knife
I could show you all that I still have this right
That's when I watched my fertilized dandelions
Fend off the flaming Dragons
The ones left smiling became my hang-ons
They were just as well, and so am I
I have a nice life here, just like everyone else
Thank you, God, and the powers that be
I've seen the other side; it looks like Hell
I prefer to remain cheap and normal

It Fits Only You

There's a gate into my garden
And you're the only one that can fit through it

It fits only to you - you're the key
As you had moved up the path
It had measured to the shape of your shoulders
and your knees

Through your steps, it shaped only to what you are
And what you appear to be

It fits only your laugh
Which from a sample
Has bred to cheer up my living room

It fits only your smile
Though which has shone only on others
Shines all day long, on my imagination

It fits only your ponderings and your levities
It fits only your courage and your creativity
It fits your body, your face and your family

It fits only your name
The one I whisper and mouth
Through my days and my evenings

And your skin, which I hold
And kiss sometimes when
I'm clutching close my pillow

It fits only you
Cause I can't imagine my future without you
Caring for me, and loving me
In the same way
I want to care for you and love you

Kirsten Brawn-Good

Nary as My Bliss May Be

Nary as my bliss may be
    tranquilled by the denuding
    I sought and thus lost everything
A deity's hand came down
    clothing my soul in whine-stained gown
    which too swift slipped to the ground
Funny, though, my form invokes
    visions of corporate chimney smoke
    burning trees and rum and coke
I'm scared, is there maybe a vulgar charge?
    assessed and battled in my war
    I lose my dress again, it falls to the floor
Above the stove, I am barefoot
    and pregnant with a multitude
    that, as like me, wade in the nude
Parading on the freezing plain
    the faults relent to speak again
    amplified on ignoble stage
In union, the naked fists do pound
    unstable, the wall boards sound
    until they chatter to the ground
Nary as my bliss may be
    save for my merry company
    we still are useful either way

No Better, Just Different

Faberge, Vanderbilt, cash stacks, loose belt.

I say, enjoy your time with imported wine.

Don't forget, though, don't go in debt, for the
domestic's just fine.

The problem is, when power condescends, which
means when one is being conceited and snobby about
the ingredients.

It may be violently responded to by an insecure plebeian.
Who claims he only wants to descend the power but
really only dreams of his own brand of ascension.

So then, after the self-righteous boot, he next
condescends, only to self-assure his pretentious
domination.

Now, you see, we ought to minimize that kind of aggressive act. Or at
least understand it.

So now, understand.

Despite how the cooper people feel, the barber does not require to have
cooper friends when he is only interested in razors.

Despite rock guitarists feeling shunned by the orchestra, the violin may
say no to the rock show only because he does not want to jump as high
as the Stratocasters.

So, that's okay.

Whoever may be snitty, have rights to their arts and budgets and taste, and need not bathe in others' fancy ablutions.

Please, unless you have some mighty fine lawyers, avoid debt and do not ply his branded monolith with pleadings.

It's so undignified!

And, by the way, he's no better, just different.

Since private parties in all levels of society are more enjoyable,

And anonymous groups are already too full,

We need only visualize the rim lightly and let go, to teach the world to find its smile.

Yes, to make at least one extra person happy, say goodbye to the snit and tie along with the spit in his eye.

And understand, he is allowed to indulge in his truth,

And please note,

Like you, he is individualistic and changeable.

The basics are required for each of us in this world.

Together are a happy pill: affordable love, food, place.

Lotus position or Chippendale, they both were designed to relieve the legs.

With 24 hours to fill, you should not assume kings are more satisfied with the way they fill them.

Even for him, like Buddha, the cream may be sour.

So, I do not think they are.

A Thanksgiving Prayer

And the diners said their prayer.
To him the greatest, to him most high, our lord,
our God, our Allah, our Jesus, our Yahweh.
And the deity chose in that moment to reply.
"For what am I to need such greeting, such supplication?
To let you know, it is your hands, your choices, your environment that prospers you. Not I.
And look about you, the social energies do abate when you ply me with such rich fare.
Do you not feel it? It is not belief; no, they downcast
their eyes in conformity.
And so, I must, therefore, then.
Forward your thanks back to them.
Your family, your friends. Your society. Those that have saved your day!
In future, dare I suggest.
To make your wishes more potent.

To spring sweeter tides wish happiness and thanks to those about you, also
You should send a letter to the newspaper editor or start up a carbon
extraction technology lab."

Upon Reflection of my Own Demise

Upon reflection of my own demise
When echo voices mute utterance
When the dark pool's surface will not oblige
When I cease to be, I will be content
Although a man for life remains unmanifest
A marital love had surfaced, was traced and had been spent
And the apples of my eye have blossomed
And I imagine the laughter of their children
And though ink within my pen remains
And my podium a thrill
I'd be satisfied if it were dry
Or if God, dear God, subdues my quill
For my tunes and poesy that lay accrued
Will, one day, breathe fire and fly
And though the damsel within my heart remains
She trembles only on realizations
So sadly, it seems her blush for a vacant romance fades
As like my candle slowly waning
And though I ache for love's rapid pace
I would not miss the momentary rapture
For I know, love lies beyond lusts' loss
There lies the value in the capture
This is the valuable, the core.
But more often, love seems maligned
A start in lust may well leave in crime
For love smit plums, oft-times prunes become
And I feel no compunction on them to dine
Although I may still have accomplishments to sow
My edifice has puffed enough fame and love and, as casual
As dandelion seeds blown on the breeze
And now my field is finished, my hand empty
But upon my grave, by default, flowers would spring
A slightly bitter healthy tea

Kirsten Brawn-Good

For the carrion that perch upon
Trees rooted in my submission
Would have fed enough again
And I'd be relieved by crow-pecked eyes
The reality of my repugnant reputation
From the monuments that stole my joy
I'd now join, unrepentant, also oblivious to
My transgressions
Of course, I'd prefer to live and wait the accolades
I would, I would, oh how I would!
I'd probably take a bow despite my best intentions
But they'd draw a shadow on my grave
And the pretty fragrant stems would sag, less bright
My curtsey would be their shame
My enjoyment, their sacrifice
Ought I to die so they can thrive?
Not from my perspective
Through it all an exuberance for life remains
The weight is lifted. I am free
Beyond 80, I am one. Inured to life. Whole complete
I speak to me, and myself speaks
Lightened for the lonesome journey
Upon reflection of my own demise
I'd miss you all, but I'd be ready

Shotgun Wedding

This may be a shotgun wedding
But they need not bring their gun
If I continued to feel you were not my type
If I felt unsure
If I did not look on you as a potential provider of happiness
They may have had to
But not in a case like this
You are my cell, and you are my food
But I am bound by me, I'm not bound by you
I would leave if I wanted to, I would leave if I wanted to

I would leave my skin on the stage and run away with my heart
An empty shell for the actor in the ideal part
Or take my skin and give the fairy tale a bone
Cause maidens have more dignity when they do not follow Prince
Charming home
Yes, I would leave if I wanted to

Yes, but, if I did leave you
I'd have to leave you for good
Give my heart to another and consume his food
Only dream of him, and never think of you
But I cannot do that
You are too good to leave, too perfect for me
When I imagine you, I swing through the breeze
If I imagined you different, though
The swing, I would AWOL
If, for instance, you displayed characteristics that I could not tolerate
Yes, in a friend, but not in a mate
If you go, DavidLeeRothing, while I sit and wait
If you were overtly playing, while I sit down here struggling
Yes, I would leave if I wanted to, I'd leave if I wanted to

Kirsten Brawn-Good

If you were openly arrogant, and expected me to swallow
If your designs don't meet the plans that my heart
yearns to follow
If I saw in you, a battling ego rather than a desirous
soul
If I saw any of those things, then, believe me, I would not hesitate to go
So, see, I am bound by me; I'm not bound by you
I would leave you if I wanted to
If I didn't want to hold hands with you, I'd be preparing to leave
So, see, there is no need to shoot, cause
You're Adam and I'm Eve

Lizard Brain

Pettiness. The penny, in fact, is worth quite a lot.
Everybody resorts to it!
Is the final notion, the slamming of the door.
The link (who is just another frail human) without
which all will fail.
It's not the car, or insurance, but it's the spark that lights your engine.
In so many cases, the picayune starts your lizard brain.
Moving around in the primal flow, destroying rationality and reason.
A grade seven gripe in an elderly person.
There is no logic where the cent will move the hour.
Mountains of fact and reason set aside.
Trigger-loaded flickered finger against the neighbor is the norm.
Perhaps he trespassed on a blade of grass.
And wedges between brother and sister, mother and daughter and son.
They are all there.
Some small stupid point unnecessarily spoken. Nervous laughter and
shame.
Yes, the mighty cent is lord above all. As the nation is run by a lizard brain.
Take God, for instance. Maybe just a thimble full.
Is the size of a black hole.
Into which I have peered into an infinite darkness.
So deep it sucks up stars.
And its vortex wants to suck me in.
And where would we be without the atom?
Or the electron and the stitches in between?
To know where the electron goes could be the solution.
But God values being mysterious, so the answer to the puzzle is unlikely
given.
Teeny things can really set one back, like a speck of sand around your
piston.
It's the itty-bitty bitcoin that turns the screw.
It's the small air intaking moment in the discussion that
you listen to.

Kirsten Brawn-Good

What is final is the straw.

A tick effortless and raw.

A tock, a missed but necessary breath.

Leads to death.

A crux of the matter, a small aching pain. That may make us blind to empathy.

A steel guitar with a slightly too-loosed string is out of tune.

Yes, a small spin is absolutely everything.

On a plane, there is such a thin membrane.

That, if torn, leads to catastrophic doom.

The fuselage the skin between air and blood.

The synapse is next to nothing. Without it, we are none.

Small is so beautiful so powerful, the devils shun.

Or it can be its opposite.

The twist that condemns the neck.

Brain stem, limbic cortex.

Second, upon second, as it rotates past the point of no return.

The seat of emotion, addiction, mood, fight, flight, feeding, fear, freezing up, orgasm.

Paeon's brain, wildly imagining an unlikely victory. Sweat, flush, directional.

I understand this street.

And little by little, I push back into myself.

But I see others now that don't at all see.

Does she love me? Does she love me not? where would we be without the petal of the daisy.

The bolt sets the wheel. Without it, the wheel falls off.

Beliefs fight beliefs into an atmospheric fire.

The Waiting

The tragedy is----we will never meet
Good one, eh?
Not too bad?
No one dies
Just unsatisfied until the light in one flickers out
Then the other
To go down in history as the love affair that never occurred
No point in sending him another smelly brassiere
No point in sending him another seven-foot wooden statue
Not even a thank you
No point in sending him love letters, and knickers
And we are both sitting there- there and here, wondering when
If or how
Year after year
So sad
He's mad
In concert, he stayed cruelly turned away
I paid $160 for a ticket, and I never even got to see his face
It wasn't just me, it was half the stadium that also didn't get
what they bargained for
But he did create some very lovely love songs!
Just listen to their Van Halen 3 album!
In consolation of his stadium performance I suppose, the beautiful CD
was written to me!

Just Staring at a Piece of Paper

Easy falls the rain
But not so easy do my words appear on my page
I block them before they get there, now, let me think now
I say
Love, family love, I love my family
Very, very, very much
My mother, my brother, my sister, her husband
and all our children
We have come together so many times
And this has been a most valuable gift!
At Swiss Chalet, shooting spitballs through the straws
Cousins ducking beneath the table
Can't you all just sit still?
And the craziness of family dinners
Crowding around the shrimp rings
In the kitchen…baking gravy, slicing turkey
Boiling peas. What's not a tender memory?
Zero
But sadly now
My mom so generous to us all
Sits in an extended care home shithole
Her new family are those that are also out of sorts
Another old lady wanders into her room
"Who's that?" my mom asks, "will you stay to visit?"
A friendly lady with a wide smile
My mom loves that!
I guess I've written something
I'm in love with my family, but not with this poem

Russia and Ukraine

Terrible behaviour
Going on
Fully a bully
Perilous
Endeavours
A war against neighbour
A hateful affiliation
Grab the land
Slay the women
Children stolen
Torturing human
Culture burning
Erased forever
Another famous artist, scientist
Scrub him down, to the ground
Corpses
Piled around
Till the names are russified
Forever war will pray on the mind
Of those Ukrainians remaining
With a fire in their belly

And I Speak with God Lightly

I'm addicted to the news.
Every morning, I spend hours reading it and watching it.
It's become my reason for being.
Hours sunk into my computer and television.
They are wearing out!
I stand up, and my butt hurts.
I wobble on my feet to the kitchen.
To drip another cup of strong coffee.
Do a few squat exercises.
And eat lemon wafers with whipped cream.
And a bowl of porridge dappled with butter.
I'm not sure if I'm learning anything, really.
And I ought to be scribbling a poem, or a tune.
Or upgrading my book chapters where needed.
But.
Instead, I pick up a book.
A nonfiction book that goes in my mind and then immediately out
again.
I love reading.
I love watching the news.
I love the angst of American politics.
I worry about Ukraine.
I wish Putin would have a heart attack and melt like
the wicked Witch of the West that he is.
Navalny would be set free.
And Russian minds would taste the wind again of battling perspectives
and superior electricity transmission.
Almost more than anything else.
I love cooking my kids' breakfast.
Or a roast beef dinner.
And my little grandson fills me with more joy than I ever thought
possible.

And through all this downtime and domestic banter I speak with God lightly.
Now that they know me better than ever.
I've proven that I am not really that clever.
Still.
My days fill.
And I am happy.
And I speak with God lightly.

I will Will its Violent Tremors Cease

I want to try and touch the world
And press it with a gentle kiss
I want to close it tight within my tender arms
And seduce it with my feminine charms
For it seems men must meet their graves
Before vengeance is done and peace pervades
Before a sweeping tenderness aspires
We must change their blood to reduce their fire
I think men feel they need to conquer, lust and fight
Where rules of honor, wrong and right
Are a meaningless spiral, there is no shame
To win, win, win the bloody game
I know that (as a generalization) a woman's
Mother's call to arms
Is a gentle thing, soft, loving, warm
A place where babies nestle at the breast
A spot of universal tenderness
She must be subtle, tactful, wise
To lure the men with gentle eyes
To a place where egos will lay down to rest
A spot of masculine loving supportiveness
Some of us will join the fight
Leave our children crying in the night
Not be meek, soft with child
But equal the man in his bloody style
Who will sustain these valiant dames
That stand alone in the steely rain?
For he will not give from a meeker place
So she must fight alone in a loveless race
But I know, I want to show pure tenderness and love
A more gentle world, that's what I dream of
I will will its violent tremors cease
And bless it with a gentle kiss

Made in the USA
Monee, IL
20 September 2024

fb9cebe9-b549-4307-9323-a6ad77899d0bR01